About the Author

Cameron Beatty is an ex-commando, former professional firefighter, literary graduate, amateur boxer, and a dog lover. His favorite pastime is to exercise for hours at a time and befriend the local foxes in his area. He prefers his shirts to be Hawaiian and his sunglasses aviators.

Indigo

Cameron Beatty

Indigo

Olympia Publishers
London

www.olympiapublishers.com
OLYMPIA PAPERBACK EDITION

A CIP catalogue record for this title is
available from the British Library.

ISBN: 978-1-80439-311-6

This is a work of fiction.
Names, characters, places and incidents originate from the writer's
imagination. Any resemblance to actual persons, living or dead, is
purely coincidental.

First Published in 2024

Olympia Publishers
Tallis House
2 Tallis Street
London
EC4Y 0AB

Printed in Great Britain

Dedication

I'd like to dedicate this book to all the kind people in my life.

1

I arrive by truck, military surplus that rattles as we all eye each other in the back, wondering who will make it – if any. It's my second time doing this and I'm not like the others. They're new and I can see it in their faces. Eyes that are eager to please. Wonder and fear.

The truck kicks up dirt, the driver tells us we're three minutes out and to exit quickly with our bags. I didn't bring one because I know they're going to take them from us anyway. It's been a year since I was here last and I'm not looking forward to it.

We pull up to a halt. Someone I don't recognize yells at us through the rear flap. Everyone hurries off and assumes a push-up position. Some instructors kick dirt in our faces and I wonder if they know about me.

They have us counting out our pushups. Twenty-one, twenty-two, twenty-three. Lower and hold. Some people give way and collapse. They are removed and run off in a group somewhere with one of the instructors. Punishments for being different are enforced around here. But I look the part which helps.

They get us on our feet and give us a log to carry. We run it up a hill, hold it above our head, echo in cadence with the instructor's mantra about a free society and protecting our rights. The afternoon sun is harsh. I didn't sleep on the truck and my headache has gotten worse.

Stress at knowing what's to follow. *Brace up, Recruit. Look lively.*

We lower the log to our shoulders and run back down the hill. This time, we're on our backs, pressing the log up and down. We raise and hold again. Someone else gives way. The instructors scream at him and he is removed. This goes on until it's dark and I have my competition narrowed down. Four remaining and I can see one is ex-military. He uses his voice too much. Too much command, too much attention. It can go either way in these situations. Depends on who's watching and who takes a disliking.

The instructors converge on him when they see him weaken. He's bigger than me. They ask him if he has the answers now. A bucket of cold water is thrown over us. My arms are cut to pieces from crawling in the dirt. Someone else gives up and he is removed.

They tell us it will be like this all night. I don't know what to believe. It wasn't quite this bad the first time around so maybe they do know about me.

We're doing chin ups now and they make us count them out. When our timing falls out, they run us to the lake. Go. Swim. At one point, I get dragged under, but I'm ready for this so I hold my breath. I let them take me down, and I don't fight it. Eventually, they let go and I'm up swimming again with the remaining three.

I'm still not sure how I should handle this and I haven't yet given anything away. I don't know exactly what they want from me. When the ex-military candidate starts going down in the lake, I have to think quickly. They know who I am and I can feel them watching me. Sink or swim. Win or lose.

So, I grab the man around his neck and pull him to the surface which brings an end to the night.

"Gentleman," a voice says behind the light, "it seems we have our crew. Welcome to Indigo."

2

It's night and I'm on sentry with the same M4 assault rifle they issued me with last time, the name 'Chase' etched into the stock, the same feel as the last time I held it. It doesn't go away. My fatigues are still wet from the aquatic drills this afternoon. An hour of drown-proofing, an hour of waterboarding, followed by practice beach insertions the director may want us do carry out at any point. Be ready for anything. Be what everyone else is not. The moonlight is bright and the wind is cold.

I'm here with one of the other candidates from our selection, the ex-military one. He's already told me his whole story. They named him Regi and I can see why. I don't think he's killed before.

We've all been issued with single bed spaces in the tent. Night times can bring with them all kinds of surprises. "Stand to, stand to, man your posts." A barrage of footsteps, a flurry of movement, trip flares and red smoke grenades assaulting the night.

Compound defence drills can be carried out at any time of day, but we are never told whether they are real. Live ammunition is carried all the time.

The sirens still send chills down my spine. I haven't heard them for some time now. It will take some getting used to.

We've been told that the director is watching us and

that our actions will form part of our ongoing assessment. We are to not get too comfortable upon completing selection, they say. Your names are in pencil, not in ink.

He'll be watching.

Regi has told me he was born for this. I nod and look out to the night sky. Everyone is born for something.

It wasn't easy getting back here and I know I'll have to demonstrate my loyalty. I don't think anyone else has ever made their way back in after leaving. When you leave, you simply disappear. I didn't leave. I escaped.

Everyone is born for something.

3

Two hours of sleep later and I'm standing at attention at the foot of my rack, my day pack prepared with emergency rations, cold weather gear, water, and as much equipment as it can carry. No bug outs here. Fight through or RV for counter assault.

Instructor Pax makes his way down the line, not really inspecting anyone except the newbies he doesn't like. I know this man from my former stint here. He is yet to speak to me. The scar has faded but still sits above his eye. Once a wounded soldier, always a wounded soldier.

He makes an example of the recruit to my left, flips his rack, kicks in his personal locker with his boot, and empties his day pack over the floor. He says, "Don't make me do this again." And the recruit gets to it.

He looks at me briefly, then moves on.

"Men, you have been here a week now." The stirring speech about to change us all. "And this will be like nothing you have ever encountered before." He allows several steps in between sentences. "You will not see your families, your wives or your pet goldfish ever again. They are part of your former lives. And your new lives have just begun." New faces harden, eager to please.

"You've been searching for something this whole time You've been searching for your place. And if you've made it this far, I can guarantee you, *this is* your place." A long

14

pause for thoughts to sink in.

"During your time here, you will be part of a movement greater than yourselves. You will train for the freedom you've been looking for. You will become instruments of warfare. You will make sacrifices for the cause of this organization, and equally importantly," he scans the tent, "for your fellow brothers. But no man will ever be above the mission of Indigo. One in. All in."

He assigns Regi as his 2IC for the week. Yes sir, yes sir, three bags full, sir. He then says, "Don't disappoint me," and tosses a flash grenade over his shoulder as he exits the tent. A barrage of bangs and white light as we grab our day packs and leg it to the track for morning PT in full battle kit. Rifles overhead, running on the spot. Orders and commands are screamed as we crawl beneath barb wire. Keep moving, newbie, and don't look them in the eye.

The compound sits in a haze on the horizon. It's my mirage, my horror, my goal, and my fear. It's what visits me at night. That compound on the hill surrounded by nothing.

Pushups begin. Lower, raise. Lower, raise.

That compound on the lonely hill. It's my vanishing point beneath the wispy clouds.

4

They've got us working on the four-wheel drives today – jobs for the new recruits to demonstrate appropriate levels of enthusiasm. Shit work for level-one shit kickers. My white t-shirt is covered with black smears. A cigarette sits behind my ear. Just a regular grease monkey tending to his duties.

Another number, another cardboard cut-out with nothing to set him apart.

Bodies move about in the background, sounds are muted. Everything seems strangely peaceful when you reach exhaustion. You could be in the middle of a gunfight and still feel tranquil. Accepting of your fate whichever way it goes.

I've been listening to the others, their stories, their reasons for being here. Some involve family deaths or breakups. Others are more political.

Anger at the government's handling of the pandemic and being sick of getting told what to do. But everyone ultimately claims this as their reason to be here. They're fighting the good fight. They're standing up for justice. Mateship, brotherhood, patriotism. But if you offer men an assault rifle, most will tell you whatever you want to hear. War games for grownups never get old.

They bring us lunch today, stew served in our issued cups canteen. I take a seat behind the others at the base of

16

a tree. Regi is impressing everyone with a tale of how he was overseas once with the military, when he reminds us that we only have five minutes left for lunch. He then looks back over to me. I nod, but he does a double-take.

"You don't talk much, do you?"

I tell him I'm not the talking type.

He lifts his chin, but nothing else gets said. I know he's watching me. I know the others are too, but they're not the ones I'm worried about.

I take another mouthful of stew. "What do you want to know?"

He takes his time. "You've been here before, haven't you?"

"Yeah. And?"

He keeps his chin lifted, but his foot begins tapping. *Which way to go now, Regi?* "What happened?"

I shrug and say I left.

What comes next sits halfway between a question and an accusation. "What's your background?"

"Caucasian."

This gets a small laugh. Regi tells us all that we should get back to work. I sit still and let him walk off with the others. *When I'm ready, Regi.*

I glance around in the breeze. Red dirt, hills and the midday sun. I know this spot well. I once ran through here in the middle of the night. Sirens whirring, fireworks dotting the night sky in my wake, and blood seeping from my temple as the megaphone blasted, "All units, kill Chase on sight." Me sitting here now, that drone of noise bouncing around in the back of my mind, thinking of that cold night and wondering when I'll have to do it all again.

5

"You are not the past, you are the future," the voice from the PA system tells us as we sink deeper into the lake. The log is becoming heavier now and we're waiting for the first person to panic. Morning drill for new recruits. Be all you can be kind of deal.

"You don't come to us prepared for the real world. You come without any real knowledge of yourself. You come to us as lost children in the desert. It's up to us to show you what you're capable of. It's up to us to show you the way."

Another brick gets added to the top of the log and we sink deeper.

Heads sit just above the water line. People start groaning. We kick furiously to stay afloat. We've become strangely acquainted with this log by now. This log holds all our hopes, our beliefs, our dreams of purpose and meaning, and we hold it up as high as we can. In this log we trust.

We sink further. The voice keeps talking.

"You will come to understand that in order to be truly free, you must let go of who you were. You have all been misled. You are not who you think you are. You are not what society wants you to be. Otherwise, you would not be here."

Regi groans for everyone to kick harder and work as a

team. He yells this out a second time. Loud voices demonstrate strong leadership.

"You will be reborn. You will be recreated. You will find your true selves within that body that has been walking around all these years pretending, acting like the other robots you've seen shuffling about with false purpose. Empty vessels wearing human suits."

The voice comes from the compound on the hill. I know the voice well. It repeats, "Empty vessels wearing human suits," lingers for a moment, then clicks off.

Pax's silhouette stands over us against the dark morning sky, dim light making its way over the horizon. A new day has just begun. He watches me watching the others. I remain silent.

Regi is the first to cave, giving us all the excuse to drop the log.

Everything crashes down around us. Complaints about us being better than that echo through the darkness. It's always important to put on a show.

We swim to the shore. People splutter and cough as we crawl out of the lake and hug the red dirt for comfort. The sharp rocks seem strangely friendly.

"Why did you fail, men?" Pax breaks his silence. "Anyone?" Everyone is smart enough by now to stay quiet.

"I cannot let you progress to the Raider Platoon until you understand the limits of your control. You wear those green bands on your arms because that's what you are. Green. If you demonstrate that you have what it takes then you can roll with the big boys. Supply runs. Night ops. Direct action assaults. This is what we're here to do. This is how we make a difference. But until then, you're green as grass and not worth shit."

He's silent for a brief moment before he barks out, "Regi!"

"Sir!"

"You're fired as 2IC. Chase, you're up. Get this shit organized." He then turns on his heel and disappears.

It seems my world just got a whole lot worse.

6

The instructions come out of me with an uncomfortable familiarity. No posturing, just words to be taken seriously, delivered in a dead tone that's missing any zest for performance. We form up in single file and begin the jog up the hill. Today will be hard and I tell them that. Don't be surprised if we turn on one another. Games to create enemies need willing players. My words falling on deaf ears, probably.

We are preparing for ops now. Pax has us implementing direct action assaults on the kill house. Dynamic entries where applicable, firing and moving to cover the distance from the tree line and green smoke grenades to cover our withdrawal. He drifts from room to room, a flicker behind the smoke. Man down, CASEVAC prior one. The sound of incoming choppers comes back to me.

Live fire drills test our nerve. "This door, this door, on me." A flash grenade sparks and four men open up on the targets. Reload on the move, maintain muzzle awareness. It's all screams and gunfire. The sounds of war echoing through the hills.

But you are only as strong as your weakest link. And when blood is in the water, the sharks will come. I ask him what his name is.

"They call me Taps."

"You look like you're having a bad day, Taps."

He winces, ruffles his hair, looks back at me like I'm not there. I tell him that it's important that he keeps up.

He nods. "Instructor Pax wants to get rid of me."

"You're not the first." We're alone, just the two of us now. The others are watching us at a distance. They can see me having this talk.

I tell him not to worry about it too much. "It's his game and he's using you at the moment. Don't waste time thinking about it, but you're going to have to make some changes. I'll help you where I can."

He begins thanking me, but I wave him off. Don't thank me yet. No heroes here.

We push through together, room clearances, live fire assaults, beasting sessions with the log to inspire us beyond our limits. Be the future not the past, they say.

Taps struggles. His weapon jams, he fumbles with his gear. A fight breaks out, but I stop it before Pax can tell me that my leadership is being brought into question and I'm failing my ongoing assessment. Nothing personal, just business.

The flash grenade explodes and we enter, flowing through the kill house like water. Four men entry there, push up the hallway, stack up here, and so on. I give instructions and they get obeyed, but I need to stay aware. I need to keep a lookout. When I'm not around, they will talk. I see Regi looking at me and I know to not get too comfortable.

But for now, it's the beginning of a team. Whether Pax likes it or not.

7

We graduate to Raider Platoon; me, Taps and Regi with a bunch of others, green arm bands replaced for black ones with skulls. The voice of the director through the PA tells us to trust the process. We are becoming a unit operating on another wavelength of which only we could understand, he says. I've understood it before. Promises of enlightenment come before the director clicks off.

A party follows in the Raider tent. Someone pulls the tent entrance aside and I enter, gear over my shoulder, enveloped into the light and noise throbbing from inside. Beer spills across me, people stand on their racks.

Cheering, whooping, plenty of menace.

Someone wearing sunglasses offers me a beer and I take it to the back corner. I look around. Jesus. What a place. This party didn't happen the first time I was here. Regi enters. He puts his gear down and makes himself known as quickly as he can.

I know these people well. Drifters looking for something, an excuse to play out a violent fantasy. It's a dark fairy tale for men who never grew up.

They look at me a certain way. It's the look that comes from rumors and questions. I was such a different person when I first came here.

There are plenty of people who didn't graduate. Some of them have been back squatted to Green Platoon. Others have just disappeared.

Taps appears next to me. He wants to talk. He tells me thank-you again, and that he was worried he might not make it across the line.

"Don't mention it."

"Where did you learn all that stuff?"

"Watched a lot of movies, I guess."

"Pax told me I barely made it."

I nod.

"He scares the shit out of me."

I tell him that he has his own agenda. Everyone here has their own agenda.

"Regi says you were the director's guard. Is that true?" Predictable questions from a predictable person.

I don't answer.

"He also says you were here in the beginning, that you helped start this place."

I cut him off. I tell him to be very careful what he says about me. "This not a fucking playground, and if you want to make it here, let me give you some budding advice. Nothing good is going to come from you painting a giant sign on yourself saying, 'I don't know what I'm doing.' Those kinds of questions are for people who will end up back in shit kicker platoon with Pax or worse yet."

Sorry, he says, sorry.

I tell him to not apologize either.

"OK." He readjusts himself, trying to look more soldierly.

"Listen, man. We've all done things for the first time. I get it. But just understand bad things can go down here from simple misunderstandings. Look around."

"OK, thanks, no, I get it." He nods fervently.

"Don't thank me."

"Right, yeah, you've said that before. I'll stop that too." It's a lot for him to take in.

The music shifts track, followed by a cheer. Raiders dance with their assault rifles. Booze and live ammo are a bad mix.

I see another newbie enter the tent. He wasn't present at the graduation ceremony, but he wears the skull on his arm. His head his bandaged and he looks around the tent slowly. Amongst the sea of jumping people, I focus in on him, his face flickering behind the limbs and assault rifles being flung about.

He looks at me, then Taps, then exits the tent. Lots of things happen in this place and I don't profess to know all of them.

The siren breaks my trance. "Stand to, stand to." A trip flare pops in the distance, the whirring alarm filling me with dread. I place my beer down. The chest webbing goes on. I action up my rifle.

Bodies are flowing out of the tent, some shirtless, some still wearing sunglasses and hats. Stand to, stand to. There's gunfire in the background. It's actually happening this time, an attack from a rival faction, probing us for weakness, testing out perimeters. Don't give away the gun emplacements, fire in short bursts and remember the RV point for counter assault if it comes to that.

We flow out of the tent, me somewhere in the middle, and leg it to our positions. The flare still burns. I see shadows in the distance, muzzle flashes, and the sound of bullets whizzing overhead. When they are closer, I hit the deck and crawl. Taps is behind me. Keep your head down, Taps. This will test you.

I stack up against the sandbags and pull at Taps until he's next to me. I peek over. Jesus. They're not just probing. They're pushing up.

I lean into Taps, right next to his ear. "Don't shoot yet. They haven't seen us."

"I don't think I'm ready for this."

Everyone feels that way, but you squeeze the trigger when you have to. We lay low, safeties off, weapons at instant and ready to fire. They get closer.

I tell Taps I'll shoot first and he says OK. Someone throws a grenade somewhere across the hills and the shockwave ripples through me. Commands are screamed out in violent muffles. They're nearly on top of us now. If I had a bayonet, I'd have it fixed.

Get ready, Taps. It's happening. I take up a fire position.

But before I can fire, the flare dies out and we're in darkness. We're operating on sound now. I can hear them. Twenty meters, maybe ten. Taps' breathing gets louder.

I hold my position. Rapid heartbeats but steady hands.

Then it all goes quiet. No commands, no gunfire. There's nothing. I scan left and right, waiting.

"What's happening?" Taps whispers.

"I don't know."

The clouds cover the moon. I can't see anything. After a long silence, there is a pop and another flare makes its way through the night sky. They are gone.

I collapse back down behind the sandbags, drenched in sweat.

"Are they still here?" Taps whispers.

"It doesn't look like it."

"Fuck." Taps pushes up next to me and we sit there together in silence for a long while.

Some radio chatter comes through. Commands for us to hold our position until further notice, followed by a status check from all callsigns. I hear them sounding off. All clear, all clear, man wounded, the usual.

Taps and I don't move. He looks down eventually and says, "I pissed myself."

"Yeah," is all I can say, "it happens."

8

A sunrise greets us the next morning as we bury the bodies, black silhouettes digging holes against the red sky, one of ours and one of theirs. Cannon fodder for the cause we're fighting for. It's quiet, but I can feel the thoughts of others.

The voice of the director tells us about the greater good. He tells us that our fallen comrade is now the past and not the future. He tells us to honor him, that his sacrifice is something we can all admire and that someday, it will become clear to us that his brave death was not in vain, but was part of the glory that we will all feel.

I remember hearing his death over the radio in the midst of the attack.

He screamed out for help.

The body gets lowered slowly into the hole, solemn faces playing the part. He was from Green Platoon. No one knew him. But heroes respect the fallen. Because in death we become everything. We become fearless. We become warriors. Until then, we're just trying.

I look around, lowered heads, reflective faces. All the respect in the world now. Green Platoon. Shit kicker platoon. Death is your short cut to acceptance.

I see Regi. I don't wonder much about his involvement last night. He plays the role well, but I know he's just thinking about the next time he'll have an opportunity to sight someone down and squeeze the trigger.

How it will go down, how it will feel? He reflects deeply with everyone else.

I'm so tired. I helped dig the hole, but I'm not a part of this. Something about the way Taps looks at me from the other side of the burial bothers me. I wait until it's over. I then head off somewhere out of sight where I hyperventilate.

It lasts maybe thirty seconds. I take a knee.

I can't go back home. My dog has died and there are probably squatters living there now too. In my mind, it's already overgrown with vines and weeds. It's gone. Life has been lawless since the pandemic. My dog has died and I'm alone.

I wish I could go back in time and speak to my younger self. I see images of me laughing and smiling. I had a dog I raised and I loved him. We ran on beaches and played. But I can't be too hard on myself. I didn't ask for the pandemic, I didn't ask to be what I am now.

There are some things I can still feel. I don't know if it's the answer, but it's the only thing I have other than survival. I want to get away. I want to be left alone. It's hard being what everyone expects you to be. It takes a toll.

I chose to start this place though, and I chose to come back. There is a piece of me here even if I don't recognize it anymore.

Another soldier with a bandaged head startles me. I snap out of it and look up at him. He doesn't speak. He stares at me long and hard. Here I am, at the base of this tree curled into myself. I am here, and everyone is over there. I am the problem. I am the one who doesn't fit.

He looks at me, silent and blank. He then reaches into his pocket and offers me a cigarette. I take one and nod. He sighs and looks back up, out to the empty sky, nodding to himself before he walks off.

"In time," the director says, "in time."

9

The stillness after battle illuminates everything. Words, expressions, and gestures are magnified. Colors seem brighter, sounds become louder in the muted aftermath. If you're not used to it, you can become paranoid. You think someone is watching you, that someone knows the truth. That thing you've been holding onto wants to eat you alive if you let it take a hold. That moment you hesitated perhaps, or that moment you failed that no one else saw but you. That morbid secret you have comes to life.

It takes a monstrous form and you see it wherever you look. It can visit you in your dreams if you're not careful. Cold sweats and waking in fright.

Anger at yourself. Anger at everyone for making you remember. That person looking you back in the mirror is not you anymore and it sends you crazy.

I volunteer for a supply run into town. You need to keep busy. The ongoing assessment never ends. Demonstrate the willingness to help and you will be rewarded.

They give me some civilian clothes, a work shirt and jeans, and a list of items, fuel cans, tools, those sorts of things. It's considered a low-level operation. There is some risk involved so they leave it to the Raiders. People out there can be hostile – rival factions, embittered people, looters, what's left the military. They issue me with a concealed holster for my 9mm handgun and some extra magazines. I take them from the Q store clerk without so much as a second look.

They're all waiting for me in the four-wheel drive, everyone with different tasks. The 9mm goes on my belt under the back of my shirt, the mags go in the pouches and I get in the car.

The drive into town is quiet. I stare out the window eying the red hills, the empty space that becomes peppered with rundown houses and burnt car skeletons as we get closer. I know one of the other Raiders. He hasn't spoken to me yet since my arrival. Cinders, they call him. The last time we saw each other, he was pointing a gun at me as the sirens whirred in the background. He sits in the driver's seat and glances at me in the rear-vision mirror. No one talks, but it doesn't bother me.

They drop me at the service station, which has become a one-stop shop for locals in the area. Cinders tells me he'll be back in fifteen minutes. He reminds me of our withdrawal plan if compromised and I say, yeah, I got it.

He says, "Good," and tears off.

I make my way into the service station. It's run down. Rust, cracked glass, empty milk crates. The attendant sees me coming and watches closely through the window. I push open the door and nod. He probably knows who I'm with, neither a good or bad thing.

I begin piling up items on the counter. Duct tape, canned food, batteries. He asks if I have cash and I tell him yes. As I hand it over, I ask if he is taking telegrams. He takes a moment before he says yes.

"There might be one for me."

"OK." He lets his eyes drop beneath the counter, then raises them again. "What name?"

I give him some initials instead.

"Right." He produces the telegram and slowly hands it over. I take it from him and stuff it in my back pocket. "Thanks."

I've timed everything so I'm not waiting around. I've counted several cars pass by whilst I've been here and one of them has double-backed. A black ute with tinted windows. I don't want to be standing here on this road any longer than I have to.

I pull the telegram out of my pocket. It's folded over and contains the letters C.S.L. on the front. When I open it, all I see is three words. *"You're all clear."*

It's dated a week ago when I was still in Green Platoon. I burn the telegram and grind it into the dirt with my heel. Cinders approaches in the distance.

He pulls to a halt in front of me. "Get everything?"

"Mission success." I load the items into the back. I think about the message, when it was written and the events that have happened since. I think about the person writing it. I do my best to envisage her, at her desk or maybe tending to a wounded Raider. It's been so long.

I try not to let my mind wander. I have to deal with this one step at a time. Before those distant feelings can come back to me, to remind me I'm still alive, that there might be hope, I slam the back door and say, "Let's go."

10

We're gathered in a mob, an empty circle formed in the middle, people cheering and a brooding quality. Everyone mills about me, a buzz of activity, bodies shoulder to shoulder and bumping into themselves as Pax makes his way to the center. *Don't act too surprised,* I tell myself.

I keep my head down, but I glance about. I can't see her, but I know she's here. Pax stops in the middle and they all fall silent. He then gives a speech. I keep looking about. There is an applause so I join in.

He keeps talking until he says they've come to a decision. He waits for a dramatic moment, but it's no shock to me when he calls my name. Surprise, surprise. They say the hardest decisions are always the right ones.

I'm in the middle of the circle now limbering up. Not too much movement. It won't make any difference. I can see him approaching through the crowd. Bodies move aside in a ripple. I see his head appear and he's much bigger than I thought.

He walks straight for me, no breaks in his stride. All I can say is, "Jesus," under my breath. And then I take him apart.

It lasts maybe a minute, a cacophony of dull thuds, some groans and a cracking noise that finishes things before a roar erupts.

People flock in, cheering, whistling. But I just keep

looking around through swollen eyes until I find her. She locks eyes with me through the crowd. I've kept this hidden from her this whole time, but now she knows.

She knows what that look means, what it's meant in the past, and what it will mean for what's about to follow.

I've come this far, but it's not time to take my mask off just yet. They keep cheering so I raise my fist.

11

I'm hurt pretty badly and I need to be carried into the med bay by Taps. He won't stop talking about the fight, but I can't think clearly. My eyes are swollen, my face is bleeding, and I think I've cracked a rib. This is the price I've paid and I hope it works. It could have been much worse.

It's been important that everyone has seen me do this. I want them to know. Regi kept away from me after the fight, as did Cinders and Pax. Didn't want to join in the cheers it seems. Everyone fights for acceptance in one way or another. Before I disappear into the compound, I see Pax rubbing his scar above his eye.

Taps is excited. He's never been in the compound before. He opens the door and I direct him through the hallways. There is no one here. We pass the director's quarters, a red door with no sign. I don't tell this to Taps.

We round the corner, me dragging my feet, Taps chatting away. I tell him I need to be quiet for a bit and he apologizes. The med bay is just up here, I say, and Taps says OK.

We make it to the door. Adrenaline and pain numb the nerves. It's all happening quickly and I'm just responding as I go. I knock on the door. She says, "Enter," and I open the door.

I see HR when I enter. Her back is to me on the other

side of the room.

She's reading something. It looks as I remember. A doctor's room from civilian world. White sheets, a patient chair, instruments sitting in hydraulic fluid. She gestures to the chair and says, "Put him down there."

Taps pulls me across the room and sits me down. She then turns around and says, "You look like shit, Soldier."

"Feel like shit."

"Well, let's take a look at you." She hasn't met my eye yet. She begins prodding, inspecting, making notes as she goes. Taps stands behind me in silence.

"These cuts don't look good." She gets some solution and gently dabs away at my face.

"Will I need stitches?"

"Maybe. Depends how well you heal yourself." She keeps dabbing. "The body is a strong thing. It has all sorts of mechanisms to repair itself. But if it's under too much pressure, these mechanisms start to fail."

"Better give me the stitches then."

"Well, we'll just wait and see. For now, we'll just keep them clean."

She leans in with a stethoscope and checks my heart. She still avoids my eye. "The good news is you're very fit. That's a very low heart rate following such an activity. The bad news is you're probably quite concussed. And there's not much I can do about that. Try not to get into any more fights over the next couple of weeks."

I nod.

She sighs. "I'm going to need some more bandages. Soldier" – she turns to Taps – "we're running low on supplies here. Can you go and source me some field dressings, please?"

"Yes, ma'am."

I thank Taps and he leaves. When the door closes, we both look at one another. She grins out the corner of her mouth. "It's good to see you."

It hits me all of a sudden, the sound of the door closing, finally being alone with her, everything leading up to this moment, the strain of it all, I guess. Holding on for so long, being wound tight. I get hit with another wave of it and I struggle to breathe.

She touches my arm and says it's OK, you're safe, you've done really well. "Just breathe. Breathe."

But I don't want to be responsible for anything else. I want her to be safe, but I don't think I can pull it off. I'm going to wreck everything. I can't do it any more. I'm grabbing at the sides of my head, I'm squeezing my eyes shut. Bad memories flooding my mind.

Her touch remains gentle. "*Ssshhhhh,*" she says. She's calm and it helps. "No one knows about us. No one knows. You are safe. We are safe."

"OK," I say, "OK." I start to come out of it. My eyes are seeping water and it stings my cuts. Hands shaky, forehead sweating. Just a bad dream playing itself out.

"We don't have much time."

"I know. It's OK. I'm OK."

"Listen to me." She gets in front of my face and holds my head in her hands. "No one knows anything. They don't know about us. They don't know that you came to get me last time."

I'm nodding as she talks, convincing myself.

"You can do this. But we have to wait for the right

time."

"I don't know how long I can hold out. They'll find out. I know it."

"Hey," she says. "No one is going to find out. You can be your own worst enemy. Don't tell yourself those things. This is only temporary."

"Only temporary," I echo.

Taps' footsteps make their way up the hall.

"Now is not the right time." She looks at me hard. "But soon. Soon, we'll get out of here together."

Taps flings open the door carrying as many field dressings as he can cradle. He then looks at HR earnestly and says, "I get can go and get more if you need it?"

12

Raider Platoon is on patrol, two scouts up the front, the rest of us in formation behind as we conduct recon in the eerie late afternoon sun. A scorched desert blows red sand in my eyes. Dead trees cast long shadows.

Our rules of engagement are loose. We fight with the government sometimes, military or police when they get too close. It used to be for a reason, but now everyone fights everyone. We occupy a lot of land and resources. Indigo seems attractive to some. Some of our soldiers used to fight against us in their previous lives before they crossed over. Now they shoot back at their own.

I haven't fired my rifle in anger yet since my last stint here, but it all still feels familiar. I hope it hasn't left me. The time to freeze is not during a gunfight. Trust your reactions, don't overthink it. The hands move by themselves under pressure. You change magazines on the move, you rectify gun stoppages as they occur. Don't overthink it.

Regi and Cinders are our scouts today up front, stopping to take a knee every so often, the rest of the platoon following like dominos. They talk to each other, and point at things. They've taken a disliking to Taps. Yesterday, they moved all his gear out of the tent and dumped it back with Green Platoon. Regi looking for a quick in with the Raiders, alliances forming on the inside.

Push out the one who threatens you. Taps is friends with me. That could be a mistake depending on who you ask. It's hard to keep up sometimes. Rules overlap other rules and it gets confusing.

A dust devil whirls its way across the blue sky. The sound of wind cuts at my ears. I think I'm losing weight.

We come to a halt again. All of us take up positions where we can, behind trees if they're around or against rocks to minimize profile. I see the glint of light reflecting in the distance as the car approaches along the road. A black ute with tinted windows. I've seen this car before.

The ute moves along the road, all of us in prone positions, tracking it with our rifles. Four hundred meters. Aim slightly above, lead by three points of aim if necessary. The car stops directly in front of us and idles.

When you've seen something before, it's easy to second guess. I have seen this car before, and now I'm looking at it again with an entire platoon staring at the same thing. They see what I see. We have stopped for this reason, yet I'm still uncertain. I haven't slept much and my mind has been racing.

Before you act, before you cross a void you can't come back from, you want to be sure. People who act too quickly haven't seen the bad side of a mistake. Tell-tale signs who you're dealing with.

I've made mistakes. I've been on the side of regret before and it haunts you. A moment you can't take back. A ripple effect around you. And when people look at you, you're convinced that's what they see.

I can see this ute now, and it seems everyone else can too. But I still doubt myself. All of us are here in this desert, lying under the sun, staring down our rifles at this ute which stares back, idling, thinking, weighing up its options.

In a second, we could have it riddled with bullets. It's amazing how much easier decisions become when you can hide behind others. One shot would do it. I felt threatened, someone would say. I saw a gun. I heard a noise. Another notch on the kill count board back at Indigo.

I feel it with everyone else. It's good and bad, the part of me I hate. The part of me that lives deep down and won't go away. To kill, Sergeant, to kill.

You need to know yourself well to keep it under control. You need to know when it will happen, when it will come out. Feed it in controlled environments, remove yourself when it rises unwelcomed. You need to think beforehand and you need to be certain. Because once that void is crossed, there is no going back.

The ute idles and we wait, fumes from the exhaust blurring the background in the heat. Slowly, it moves on.

You need to be certain.

13

A bonfire burns in front of us as we wait, everyone crowded around on this cold night, flickers of light fading outside the fire and keeping us in the dark.

Soldiers smoke weed and drink booze. Headbands, war paint, sunglasses at night. Someone pops a red smoke grenade and tosses overhead. The red haze envelops us. Smokey outlines appear and disappear. Tonight is a big night.

Tonight, we wait on the director.

I'm somewhere in the middle, watching, being still. I hear someone mention they thought they saw the black ute earlier today. They are going to find that black ute and blow it pieces, they say. IED on the road. Send it up to heaven in blast of fragmentation.

The life of this place feeds itself somehow. Bodies morph into one, a life force that sways and pulses. Someone behind me says they know me.

"You're that guy, aren't you?" He raises his fists in boxing pantomime.

"Yeah, I'm that guy."

He ducks and weaves behind his fists. "Nice." His face keeps changing. "Hey" – he rests his forearm on my shoulder – "hey, man. I gotta ask because it's on my mind. You know how it is. Did you serve in Special Forces with the director back in the day?" He gestures with his other hand. "Before all of this?"

I don't answer.

"Aw come on! OK," he says, "OK, I get it." He raises his palms. "I'll back off. Relax." He goes to pat me on the shoulder, but then stops himself.

Jittery, feverish. "Oh. One more thing though. Did you run out on us last time? Because that's what they've been saying. Disappeared. Vanished. Puff of smoke. Gone."

I tell him I had to go home to feed my goldfish. "*Ha!*"

I wait for him to go but before he does, he leans back in and says, "Better not do it again, tough guy."

A frosty reception. The mob decides your fate. I stare deep into the bonfire.

Taps appears next to me. He tells me that Regi has been intimidating him and he doesn't know what to do. I say being around me won't help. I can't help him. I'm not here for that.

He's shit scared. "He's following me. I know it. He's up to something. Him and Cinders."

I tell him he has to get away from me. You have to choose sides.

Decide who you want to be. Weigh up the cost. I tell him he has to go away now. Taps looks around aimlessly, goes to say something, reconsiders, then disappears somewhere into the night.

This is when I see the director. It's only an outline, and he never comes into the light. He appears behind the bonfire and everyone cheers.

"Soldiers," he says once the cheering stops, "men. Warriors of Indigo. Tonight is a special night. Tonight is a night of baptism."

I look around. I can see the outline of HR behind the director. She remains a shadow.

"There is danger on the trail, men. Lurking, burrowing, creeping danger. It's everywhere. Its skin is cold. Its heart is black." There are lengthy pauses between sentences. He breathes deeply. The outline of his face flickers in the fire. "They will say things about us out there. They will say we have lost our way. But I would expect that much from them. They want to control our rights but don't want to control their own actions. They restrict our food and try and take away our weapons. They prod us with sharp-ended spears but don't want us to flinch. They are the liars that will bring this world upon itself. They are empty vessels walking around in human suits. Empty, immoral beings. Bastard sons of the pandemic."

He falls silent. All we can hear is the fire crackling.

"Men," he says, "tonight, we celebrate our independence."

A soldier with a bandaged head appears. Another one, a different one. He moves mechanically, dragging a blindfolded man. He stops in front of the fire and pushes the man to the ground.

"Tonight, someone will complete their training."

The crowd comes to life a little. I hear some talking to my left. Pax appears in the light of the fire. He points into the crowd and after a while Taps moves forward. Pax gives him a gun.

"Tonight, we will all become closer."

Taps takes the gun. The man in the dirt whimpers, cross-legged. Taps says something to Pax, but Pax shakes his head. The crowd starts chanting.

Cinders comes into the light and grabs Taps by the back of his neck. He pushes his head forward and raises the gun for him. The chanting grows louder.

Taps' hand shakes. I know he won't do it, and they do too. Keep the one you don't like down. Keep him humiliated. Hate in him what you hate in yourself.

Taps doesn't do it. The crowd boos and Pax snatches the gun from him.

Cinders takes him off somewhere. Boos and taunts. Fear and horror.

"It is shame," the director says once the crowd falls quiet, "when the hypocrisy is exposed."

Pax points again. This time, Regi appears. He takes the gun and I look into his eyes. He grins, but I see fear. Come on now, Regi. Now is not the time for weakness. Be what they want you to be. Don't grow a conscience. Show them you're not scared by succumbing to your own fear of rejection.

The gun gets raised. He pauses. It's a long pause. The shaking starts with him too. Regi lowers the gun and the crowd boos.

Pax stares at him long and hard. All he has to do is shake his head slowly, a stern look of judgment. You have let me down. You are not one of us. You have failed. It's simply a look. No words needed.

And with that, Regi raises the gun and blows the man's face apart.

14

A full moon, a rain storm, and wild soldiers dancing around a dying bonfire. A lifeless body carried away above a sea of Raiders like ants with an insect. My days here are limited. I sleep with one eye open and a hand on my rifle. I jump at noises in the night.

They have put Taps in the cage where they taunt him. Regi joins in. Cinders grins, Pax approves. I have kept my distance because they will turn on me. My efforts will only get me so far. Soon I will have to make another move to keep them at bay. I will have to go further than before. I don't know how much I have left in me to give. The mask is wearing thin and I fear the house of cards will crumple.

Indigo is changing. I started this. This is my work. It used to be small.

It used to be controlled. Now it's taken on a life of its own and no one can stop it. The director sits in the compound and tells us to embrace our demons.

He tells us we have been fed lies. He tells us when he was in Afghanistan he saw children more savage than our own soldiers kill men like it was nothing. When he was in Afghanistan, he says. The best and worst time of his life, he says.

I don't see HR much. She is confined to the compound where she patches wounded Raiders back together in the med bay. She was a doctor before the pandemic did this to

47

us. She fixes things. I tried to get her out of here last time, but I failed. I set the fireworks in the distance, lit the fuse and ran, Raiders staring up vacantly at the night sky. Soldiers, robots. Dead men with able bodies, a signal to my contact in town. The operation is a go. Get the keys, get the car and RV ASAP.

I tried as hard as I could, but I had to leave her. Pax still rubs the scar above his eye when he looks at me. Wounded soldier with an agenda. But I keep clear for now.

There is a time for everything.

15

I'm on a supply run with some of the Raiders, four rag tag soldiers in a beaten-up Jeep, rifles out the windows and orders to shoot on sight anything that poses a threat. The rules of engagement have changed. We are in hostile territory, the director says. It is all-out war now. No more civilian attire.

Military fatigues show who we are. We're at high readiness. Scan for threats and call in reinforcements if necessary.

They drop me at the service station again, but this time they leave a soldier with me. He is new from Green Platoon and I tell him to wait at the door. The attendant sees me coming and produces a package on the counter, a box covered in brown paper. He asks what the hell is going on back there.

I don't answer, but I tear a small hole in the paper. It's full of general anesthetics. "It wasn't easy getting a hold of this stuff. What the hell do you need it for?"

I tell him I just follow orders and I pay him what he's owed. I look out at the soldier by the door. He's wearing a hat, but I can see bandaging around his head underneath.

I ask the attendant if he has any telegrams for me. He gives me a piece of paper and I move away to the aisles. *"By the tree, 2300 hrs,"* it reads. It's dated today. I tear it up and drop it in the bin.

A car is coming. When I move to the window, I see the black ute. I follow it across to the next window, but it's already gone. I knock on the window and signal the soldier. He doesn't react, just stares through me.

I move up on the attendant. "The black ute," I say, "who is driving it?"

"Huh?"

"Who are they with?" I ask. "Whose team?"

"What ute?"

"The one that just passed. It's always on this road, driving up and down."

He laughs so I grab him by the collar. I stick my handgun in his face. Don't fuck with me. "Are they with you? You planning on rolling us one of these days?"

He sinks down to the ground against the wall. He throws his hands out. "I don't know what you're talking about, man. Fuck. Don't shoot me, Jesus."

"I'm not fucking about." I move my other hand by the end of the barrel to shield my face from the blood spatter. I scream, "Tell me about the black ute."

"I don't know," he yells, "I don't know. Please. Don't shoot me. I work on my own. I don't know anyone. No one even fucking talks to me. It's just me on my own in this shit hole. Don't shoot."

I keep the gun there, but I think he's telling the truth. I glance over my shoulder. The soldier just stares. I say, "Fuck," and let him go. I grab the package under my arm and leave. The ding of the doorbell sounds behind me.

Outside, I ask the soldier if he caught the license plate of the ute but he doesn't know what I'm talking about. "I didn't see anything."

I look back at him, searching his face for answers. "What's with your head?"

"I had an accident."

"Yeah, what kind?" I go to remove his hat but he swats my hand away.

"I had a problem," he says. "And now it's fixed."

16

We meet by the lone tree in the center of the horizon, a clear night sky scattered with stars. Wildlife surrounds us. Birds flap their wings in their nests. Possums watch us from branches. Somewhere, a dingo trots across the desert. Wonders of the universe in a place of war.

She gets closer and stops in front of me. I don't see her face. She looks at my injuries in the night, moves my head gently aside as she touches my face, runs her hand over my ribs and feels for something. There is the sound of four-wheel drives in the distance, but at the moment it seems only like a soothing hum. Fatigue and untapped emotion make me this way. Your lens changes.

I tell her that I can't stay at Indigo much longer and she says she knows. But it won't be like last time. She says she can come with me.

I don't know where we would go, or what's left out there. I see a beach in my mind. I see Banksia trees, gum leaves, sand. Somewhere quiet and away because I'm tired of all this.

I've been fighting for so long now. Wars, people, my own conscience in conflict with itself. It doesn't end. There is no light at the end of the tunnel. You fight because you think it will bring you peace, but it doesn't. I know this. I would tell this to my younger self if I could. Don't start because it doesn't end. Your world becomes smaller. You kill off other parts of yourself and it's not until it's too late that you look back and think that you'd wished you'd done things differently. I don't want to be a killer but sometimes it's all I can feel. The problem becomes my solution.

She says it's OK, she understands, that I'm safe with her. She sees me for what I really am. I can breathe now, and whilst this moment will be short and I know I'll have to go back to Indigo wearing my mask and my soulless front, a projected image of all the things I hate, I do my best to feel the peace this brings. Something opens up inside. Barriers are pulled down and it flows through me. Relief, hope, love. Worlds collide. Trees sprout from dead soil. Rain floods wash away old bones. I am here, I am present, I exist. And maybe if things stay the way they are with me, I'll at least be able to look back and remind myself of this time. Grab the moments when you can.

She says everything will be OK and I let myself believe her, even if it's not true. She has a plan. She will draw them in and when the fighting starts at the Indigo borders, we will make a move. The director has lost his mind and Indigo will turn on itself. It's time to move on, it's time to be free.

I don't ask about the anesthetics. I don't ask about the bandaged soldiers I've seen walking around because I don't want to ruin this.

When the fighting starts, come and get me, she says. I'll be there.

17

Taps lies in his cage as people move about him in the background with a dull sense of activity, his bruises and bloodied face of no consequence to the blurred images of soldiers carrying out menial tasks, his suffering as commonplace as their daily chores. They have turned on him and this is what happens. If you're not one of us, you're one of them. A message to those who don't conform. Middle ground doesn't exist.

They haven't fed him much and he looks emaciated. There are graffitied symbols over the wooden cage, a peace sign, a snowflake, and all kinds of lettering. "Abandon hope." "Feed me blood." "No kills. No mercy."

I approach slowly and take a knee by the cage. He's lying on his back, propped up by the wooden bars made from branches. He doesn't react to me, just stares ahead into nothing.

I keep my voice low. I ask him how he's holding up, but he doesn't answer. Cinders is watching me, but I don't care now. The clock ticks and I make my plans.

I give taps some rations through the bars. He's still not moving so I tell him I'm placing inside the cage, and to keep it hidden.

Eventually, he talks. "What would you do?"

I think about what he's asking. I think about times when I've had to prove myself, times when I've had to

54

make hard decisions. Above all, I think about how I've lost touch with who I am. My grinning face as a young kid. The things I can't do anymore. The people I've let down.

I tell him I can get him out of here, if that's what he wants. I don't tell him when. I don't mention HR, but I tell him I have a plan.

"This wouldn't happen to you," he says.

I tell him to not be too certain. "I'll come and get you." I touch his shoulder through the bars. "Just hold on a little longer."

"Where would I go?"

"I don't know. You could come with me if you wanted."

He nods gently. "All this has meant nothing." Taps says, "I came here and worked hard and this has happened. All this has meant nothing."

I look at him through the bars. I've seen this look in people before. The spirit goes. "You don't need this place. You're not like these people."

"Looters killed my family," he says. I nod.

"It's gone. All of it. Gone. Nothing." His voice trails off and he stares at the roof of the cage. "I need to make it mean something."

"You won't be able to. You can try, but you won't."

"Where did you see yourself?"

"When?"

"Before you came here."

"I used to picture myself moving on to other things I guess. Instead, I became stuck."

"Stuck," he echoes.

"Yeah."

"At least you got somewhere." He breathes in deeply and exhales.

"They told me they'd feed me to dogs." He musters a chuckle which morphs into fighting back tears.

"Hey," I say, "we're going to get out of here. Both of us. I'll get your rifle back. No one is going to touch us."

Taps screws his face up and squeezes his eyes shut. He clenches his jaw. Shut out the pain.

"Just hold on. A little longer." He nods.

I have to leave him this way because they're starting to notice. As I rise to my feet, Pax makes eye contact with me. He runs a finger along his neck like a knife.

We'll see about that.

<h1 style="text-align:center">18</h1>

I'm perched in the tree line near the compound when the fighting starts, a man on a knee with a rifle across his back and a shadow stretching across the land. Tonight, I am a predator. "Stand to, stand to." Trip flares pop in the distance, the siren whirrs. A sentry fires in three round bursts at an enemy pushing up on their position. Bodies flood out of the tents as the director's voice tells us that we all know who we really are in the moment of truth.

Death before cowardice. Blood before peace.

The compound looms in the distance. My horror, my goal, my nightmare. The outline of HR moves by the window of the med bay. Come and get me. Now is the time.

The sounds of war accompany my movement between the trees. Distant screams for a medic, gun fire and frag grenades. It's a cold night. Everything hurts more in the cold.

I'm in the jungle of my own mind. Branches snap across my face as I run. I leap and duck and the background flashes with battle. Pax patrols the compound. Pax. A wounded soldier with an agenda.

He stands guard by the door listening to the radio chatter. Calls for reinforcements are made. Send everyone. But he still stands guard.

I take the long way around, behind the ridge line of

the hill. I keep my eyes on him. He patrols up and down, pausing at the corner. This will be the rhythm of his death. Touch that scar, Pax. One more time.

I make it to the wall of the compound. In a crouch, I slowly move up on him. He appears around the corner, turns and disappears again. I can feel it in me. I can see its face. My other half. Staring me down, coming to life.

You're in my world now, Pax. Touch that scar and remember because I'm going to do it right this time. I snatch him around the neck and pull him away from the window. He reaches for his hand gun, but I throw it away. He knows it's me.

I let this realization sit with him for just a moment. I am the one, Pax. This is how it ends for you. I feel his fear and his regret. It's all amounted to this. I then stick the knife in his neck and he gurgles.

The body goes in the bushes and I switch back to my rifle. I move up on the door. Single man room clearances from here on. I push open the door and make entry. Hallway clear, thirty feet to the end. I make my way down, rifle at the ready. Distant explosions cause the lights to flicker. Plaster dust falls down on me.

This place. I remember this place. *Let's start it together, Chase, let's fight back.* His voice drones through the PA system. A running voice over for the battle at hand. "They want us to think for ourselves but they treat us like children. But the children will grow. A child never forgets. Their hands remember the pain. The hand that feeds us."

I stop outside his door. I can hear him breathing. He sits there and watches his men die. He knows as well as I do. There is no end.

I make entry to the med bay, two steps in the direction of most likely threat, and scan the room. HR stands in the corner, arms by her sides. She's been waiting.

"Come on," I hold out a hand as I check the hallway. "Let's go."

But she doesn't move. We look at each other for a moment. Her eyes are sad. I move towards her. I let her move my rifle to the table as she hugs me. "I just want to have this moment," she says.

She hugs me tight. The lights around us seem to dim. The gunfire fades away and it's just us here in the middle of the room. "I knew I could rely on you. I just want this moment before anything else happens."

I see the stars of our last visit. I see the beach in my mind. Blue skies somewhere. Peace. I share this moment with her. She holds on. When she lets go, I take my time turning around. Taps stands in the doorway. And Regi stands behind him.

I take in this image. And now I see. I look into Taps' eyes. His look contains everything. Shame, fear, anger, horror. Regret and sorrow simmer beneath the surface. It's the look of his new beginning. This is the man he wants to be. They'll bring him back into the Raiders after this for sure. He will kill, he will fight.

I beeline on Regi. I back him up against the wall and let my fists go. He can't handle it. I plant my feet and keep throwing. He has no answer. It's not the same as executing someone who is unarmed, Regi. But the lesson is short-lived. Taps piles on and hugs my arms to my sides.

I'm on the ground now and it's Regi's turn. Taps holds me from behind as Regi gets his punches in. Blood flies. I splutter and struggle to breathe.

That's it, Regi. Make the most of it while you can. Play the part. Tell the story later about how you saved Indigo.

HR stops it and I catch my breath. Taps keeps a hold on me from behind.

Eventually, I look up.

She says it doesn't have to be this way. But she knows me better than that. "I needed to be certain," she says, "and I'm sorry. But Indigo can't go on like this. There is no future in it."

Blood runs down my face, filling my eyes.

"We're going to be overrun tonight. And we're going to join forces with them. Because it's the only way. Everything is crumpling and we need to think about a stable future. Stable being the word."

She turns her head and listens to the director's voice for a moment. "You can replace him. The men will follow you. You can be that person. You've been that person once before."

I shake my head. She waits a long moment before she nods. She then turns and moves to the table behind her.

"I'm sure you've noticed the bandaged soldiers by now." I can hear her fumbling about with her back to me, opening draws, the clinking of instruments. "You picked up some items for me the other day actually. It's a crude procedure, but it works. You remove the right part of the brain and they become very obedient. They lose personality and the ability to make moral decisions. But with right guidance, they can be used very effectively."

She turns around with a needle. "I don't want to do

this," she says. "I don't want to lose you. But we do need you. So, I need to say this one more time. Please. We can run this place together."

I just look back at her and she says, "OK."

It's a long walk across the room. The needle glints in the light. I think of everything. My journey here, my upbringing, the time before the pandemic.

I was a kid in my backyard playing with frogs from the local river. I went to school and wore a uniform. I tried to get people out of the street when the riots started. Someone told me I reminded them of their son.

Memories and feelings. Love and loss. Decisions and consequences.

I've lived the best I could. I've tried. You can be hard on yourself because in those moments you see it that you are the one to blame. It all comes down on you and you sit up late at night thinking about it. But there comes a peace with letting go. You can't fight forever; you can't help everyone. This world knows that. This world understands and if you go deep enough, you will too. The bubble breaks and you see it's not as easy as you thought.

We all have bad in us, it's just the way it is.

HR looks at me and she applies the needle to my vein. And as she pushes down on the plunger, I hear the director's words in my ears.

"An empty vessel in a human suit."